ADVENTURES
~AT~
HOUND HOTEL

PICTU...
A Capstone Imprint

Adventures at Hound Hotel is published by Picture Window Books
A Capstone Imprint
1710 Roe Crest Drive
North Mankato, Minnesota 56003
www.capstonepub.com

Library of Congress Cataloging-in-Publication Data
Sateren, Shelley Swanson, author.
Homesick Herbie / by Shelley Swanson Sateren; illustrated by Deborah Melmon.
pages cm. — (Adventures at Hound Hotel)
Summary: Alfie Wolfe and his twin sister Alfreeda enjoy helping out at the family's
Hound Hotel—but this time they have very different ideas about what to do with a
Yorkshire terrier suffering from separation anxiety.
ISBN 978-1-4795-5897-1 (library binding)
ISBN 978-1-4795-5901-5 (paperback)
ISBN 978-1-4795-6191-9 (ebook)

1. Yorkshire terrier—Juvenile fiction. 2. Dogs—Juvenile fiction. 3. Separation
anxiety—Juvenile fiction. 4. Kennels—Juvenile fiction. 5. Twins—Juvenile fiction.
6. Brothers and sisters—Juvenile fiction. [1. Yorkshire terrier—Fiction. 2. Dogs—
Fiction. 3. Separation anxiety—Fiction. 4. Kennels—Fiction. 5. Twins—Fiction.
6. Brothers and sisters—Fiction.] I. Melmon, Deborah, illustrator. II. Title.
PZ7.S249155Ho 2015

813.54—dc23   2014022989

Designer: Russell Griesmer

Printed in the United States of America.
102017   010892R

Homesick Herbie

by Shelley Swanson Sateren

illustrated by Deborah Melmon

TABLE OF CONTENTS

ADVENTURES AT HOUND HOTEL

IT'S TIME FOR YOUR ADVENTURE AT HOUND HOTEL!

At Hound Hotel, dogs are given the royal treatment. We are a top-notch boarding kennel. When your dog stays with us, we will follow your feeding schedule, give them walks, and tuck them in at night.

We are always just a short walk away from the dogs — the kennels are located in a heated building at the end of our driveway. Every dog has his or her own pen, with a bed, blanket, and water dish.

Rest assured . . . a stay at the Hound Hotel is like a vacation for your dog. We have a large play yard, plenty of toys, and pool time in the summer. Your dog will love playing with the other guests.

HOUND HOTEL WHO'S WHO

WINIFRED WOLFE
Hound Hotel is run by Winifred Wolfe, a lifelong dog lover. Winifred loves dogs of all sorts. She wants to spend time with every breed. When she's not taking care of the canines, she writes books about — you guessed it — dogs.

ALFIE AND ALFREEDA WOLFE
Winifred's young twins help out as much as they can. Whether your dog needs gentle attention or extra playtime, Alfreeda and Alfie provide special services you can't find anywhere else. Your dog will never get bored with these two on the job.

WOLFGANG WOLFE
Winifred's husband pitches in at the hotel whenever he can, but he spends much of his time traveling to study wolf packs. Wolfgang is a real wolf lover — he even named his children after pack leaders, the alpha wolves. Every wolf pack has two alpha wolves: a male one and a female one, just like the Wolfe family twins.

Next time your family goes on vacation, bring your dog to Hound Hotel.

Your pooch is sure to have a howling good time!

⌁ CHAPTER 1 ⌁
Dumb Clothes on Dogs

I'm Alfie Wolfe, and there's one thing I hate. Bows on dogs.

Another thing I hate — teensy little clothes on teensy little dogs. Have you ever seen a dog in clothes? Some dog owners are crazy! Boy or girl dog, doesn't matter. It's weird how people dress them up.

Anyhow, you won't believe what Herbie was wearing the first time I saw him. I never felt sorrier for a dog.

Herbie checked into Hound Hotel last year. Last summer to be exact. Last July to be exacter.

My dad had just left for a whole month. His longest wolf-study trip yet. Man, I missed him. But that's beside the point.

Back to Herbie.

Sure, he's not the only dog that's come to our place wearing stupid clothes. But he goes down in history as the *worst*. Trust me.

I always try to take off dogs' bows and junk, right after their owners leave. But my sister has fast fingers. (She has fast everything, if you want to know the truth — hands, legs, mouth.) I turn my back, and she's put those stupid bows right back on the dogs.

Here's the thing: every kind of dog in the world came from wolves. Every dog's

great-great-great (add a bunch more greats here) grandparents were wolves. Would you put a pink dress and bow on a wolf?

If your answer is no, here's a high five. If your answer is yes, I feel super sorry for your dog.

But back to Herbie. I'll tell you all about him, whether you put bows in your dog's hair or not.

Herbie showed up on a Friday morning. The day had started out normal. Spot, our rooster, woke me up the second the sun rose. I woke up in a bunch of pillows on the living room floor. Being asleep on the floor is normal, in the summertime anyhow. It's normal for my mom and sister, too.

We'd fallen asleep watching another dog movie. Mom was on the couch, stretching. Alfreeda was beside me on the floor, drooling all over a pillow. My sister drools as much as a bloodhound. *Ugh*. Disgusting!

I poked her awake, and we got right up. You can't be lazy when you run a dog hotel.

We ate breakfast on the kitchen floor. That's normal at our place, too.

Mom was writing another book about dogs. Like usual, the kitchen table and chairs were covered with her writing stuff.

We wolfed down our cereal. I dropped my bowl in the sink.

Alfreeda put hers in the dishwasher. Then she wiped milk off the counter super fast. And swept crumbs off the floor. And emptied the dustpan into the trash can. And hung the broom where it belongs.

She did all of that in about two minutes flat. She wasn't even panting. She's just that fast.

"Good girl, Alfreeda!" Mom said. She patted my sister on the head.

Not once.

Not twice.

Three times, as if Alfreeda had just fetched a stick from the far side of a canyon in two minutes flat. *Ugh.* My sister! Always trying to be top dog around our place. I hated it!

I dropped my bowl into the dishwasher. It landed kind of crooked.

"Good boy, Alfie," Mom said.

I got one pat on the head.

Mom handed us our dog brushes for our poodle-like hair. Our hair is super thick and curly and crazy. You can't get a comb through it, and it's really hard to brush.

So my sister and I use dog brushes — the big kind that can handle big grooming jobs on big furry dogs. Those big brushes are the only things that can handle our hair.

Alfreeda and I always race to finish first. I won't say who always wins. But you can probably guess.

Well, I can't help it. My brush always gets totally stuck, and Mom has to come to my rescue.

Somehow, Alfreeda's brush just speeds through her hair. She even has time left over to put in bows and clips and junk.

Like I said before, I hate bows on dogs. But I'm kind of glad my sister wears them. Or else we'd look almost totally alike. *Ugh!*

Finally, Mom said, "Good enough." She put down my brush.

She clapped her hands together, like she does at the start of every business day.

"All right, gang!" she said. "We've got some wonderful four-legged visitors waking up to another day. What kind of day are we going to make for them?"

"Fun," I said.

"The best ever!" Alfreeda shouted.

Mom smiled at her, super wide. She patted Alfreeda on the head again.

Suddenly Mom's cell phone rang. She grabbed it off the charger.

"Hello!" she said, cheerful as always. "This is Hound Hotel. Winifred Wolfe speaking. How may I help you?"

Mom told a dog owner how to find our place. Then she said, "We can't wait to meet Herbie! See you soon! Goodbye."

"Who was that?" I asked.

"Ms. Frill," Mom said. "Her little Herbie is going to stay with us for the weekend. She called to say they are on their way. Herbie's a little Yorkshire terrier."

"A Yorkie!" Alfreeda cried.

Trust my sister to know that kind of terrier's nickname.

"We've never had a Yorkie here!" Alfreeda shouted and jumped around. "They're the cutest little dogs in the entire world!"

She stopped jumping. She turned to me.

"I call Herbie," she said in her top-dog voice. "I get to play with him first."

"No!" I said. "I do!"

A dog that little would be a big blast. He could ride in my toy rocket. And we could play camping. I could make him a sleeping bag out of one of Dad's wool socks!

"Don't be silly, you two," Mom said. She

headed for the back door. "There's enough of Herbie to go around. Besides, he's going to stay with us for three days."

Alfreeda narrowed her eyes at me. "No," she whispered in my ear. "There won't be enough of that little dog to go around. Game on. Race you!"

We tore down our long driveway, all the way to the kennel building.

I won't say who slapped the front door first.

CHAPTER 2
Herbie Boo Boo

The race didn't stop at the front door. Alfreeda charged through the kennel building. I tore after her.

Through the office. Down the hall. Past the storeroom. Through the laundry room. Past the kitchen. Through the grooming room.

Alfreeda dashed into the big room at the back of the building. That's where all of the dog pens are. (Or you can call them kennels. Take your pick.)

I won't say who got there first. But that someone yelled, "I win!" and woke up all the dogs.

They jumped off their beds and started to bark.

"Hey, guys," I said.

"Good morning, you wonderful, beautiful creatures!" Alfreeda called to them.

She beat me to the MP3 player.

"Play some jazz music," I said. "The blues. That'd be cool."

"No," she said. "It's a sunny day. Our guests need happy wake-up music!"

She says that every morning, even if it's raining. It's annoying.

I like the blues. My dad does, too. Man, I sure missed him.

My sister was already on top of a chair. She reached to the shelf and poked buttons on the player. She *always* played the same dumb pop song.

I just stood there and watched. It's not like I could've shoved her off the chair. That would've gotten me into the doghouse for a long time-out. And I wanted to play with that Yorkie!

The song started. I groaned. The words went like this: "Oh baby. It's a sunshiny day. A baby-blue-sky day. Together baby, you and I, we're happy. So happy, happy, happy . . ."

The singer sings "happy" about twenty times. Then he sings all of the words over again. Then he sings "happy" about twenty more times after that. I'm not kidding. A dog could've written that song.

"Thank you, Alfreeda!" Mom called. She was

busy feeding the dogs their breakfast. "I love that tune. It starts the day on such a cheerful note. Play it again!"

Man, I wanted to plug my ears. But I needed my fingers for chores. Alfreeda and I had to fill the dogs' water dishes. The race was on.

Alfreeda leaped from pen to sink. From sink to pen. She filled six water dishes in about six minutes flat. I almost filled one. I can't help it. I'm a little clumsy, and I trip and spill sometimes. Give a guy a break.

Mom always makes me wipe up the floor. I was still wiping when Alfreeda called, "Finished!"

I couldn't believe my eyeballs. She had Herbie's pen all ready! A little bed sat in the corner. There was a little Hound Hotel blanket on top — folded just right. The little water dish was nice and shiny clean. Of course it was filled right to the top with nice fresh water. There was even a little pillow with a tiny bone-shaped treat on top. It was just waiting, nice and tasty, for our little hotel guest.

She'd even made a sign. It said:

WELCOME HERBIE!
I LOVE YOU SO MUCH
ALREADY!
YOUR NEW BEST FRIEND
☺ ♥ Alfreeda ♥

The letters weren't even messy.

"No fair," I said. "I don't have time to make a sign."

That second, the office doorbell rang. It sounds like a barking dog: *Yip! Yip! Yip!* You can hear it all over the kennel building. All of the dogs started to bark again. They always do when the doorbell rings.

Of course Alfreeda beat me to the office. I had to finish wiping up the stupid floor.

When I got there, she was already sitting on the bench. That's where guests sit. The human ones. Their dogs usually sit on the floor.

Mom sat at the desk, behind her computer.

A teensy doggie suitcase sat on the desk. I'd never seen one so small.

Sitting at the other end of the bench was a tall fancy lady. Ms. Frill, I figured.

Ms. Frill wore a sparkly hat with a feather on top. She had a sparkly dress and shoes that matched too. Those fancy shoes had super-high heels. She sure was a tall lady to have such a short dog.

Ms. Frill's purse sat beside her on the bench, between Ms. Frill and Alfreeda. The purse was big and pink and sparkly. A tiny dog's head stuck out the top. It looked like a toy. I mean, *he* looked like a toy. But he was real, all right. And he had a big blue bow on top of his tiny head.

He wore a teensy collar that said "SWEET BABY" on it. Alfreeda went all ooey-gooey.

"Oh, Herbie," she cooed in her talking-to-babies voice. "You're *soooo* cute! I just knew you would be!"

She rubbed her nose against his. Disgusting! Not Herbie's nose. My sister's!

"Can I hold him?" Alfreeda begged. "Please?"

Ms. Frill took Herbie out of the purse and put him on her own lap. She held him tightly and patted his head.

That's when I started to get really grossed out.

Herbie wore a blue, baby-size T-shirt. It had sparkly silver letters on the front that said "MOMMY'S BABY."

I was too disgusted to talk.

"I'm *sooo* afraid my darling angel is going to miss me *sooo* much," Ms. Frill said in a talking-to-babies voice. "Aren't you, Herbie Boo Boo? I just know you'll be *sooo* homesick. Oh, my darling baby, boo hoo…"

Mom was standing beside Ms. Frill now. Mom patted her shoulder. Ms. Frill sniffed. Mom handed her a tissue. Ms. Frill blew her nose. She handed the tissue back to Mom. Mom smiled her anything-for-a-guest smile.

"Don't worry, Ms. Frill," Alfreeda said. "I'll keep Herbie company the whole time you're gone. I'll play with him every minute. I'll make sure he isn't lonely!"

"Thank you, dear," Ms. Frill said. She shook her head sadly. "But I've never left my baby for this long. This is *sooo* hard for both of us, isn't it, Herbie Boo Boo?"

She kissed him about twenty times all over his face. She kissed his paws, too.

Suddenly I didn't want to play with Herbie anymore.

Nope.

I wanted to *rescue* him. From his life.

CHAPTER 3
Unpacking the Teensy Suitcase

Ms. Frill just wouldn't leave. She'd cry *good-byyyyyye* to Herbie. She'd go out to her car. Then she'd come right back to the office to say good-bye again!

She did that five times!

Every time, she'd say something ooey-gooey like, "When you get lonely for me, Herbie darling, just look at my picture."

Mom went to the storeroom for another box of tissues. The trash can was overflowing with used ones. Finally, Mom took hold of

Ms. Frill's arm and personally walked her to her car. Then Mom personally helped Ms. Frill into her car. She gave her one last tissue. Then Mom stood right in front of Ms. Frill's car door, so Ms. Frill couldn't get out.

Alfreeda stood at the window with Herbie, watching it all. She held Herbie and his teensy suitcase. For some reason, Ms. Frill had handed both to my sister instead of me!

The only thing Ms. Frill had handed to me was a little piece of paper. It was a new-visitor form. Ms. Frill's fancy writing covered it. There was lots of information about Herbie written all over it.

I didn't understand Ms. Frill. Why hadn't she put Herbie in *my* arms, huh? I was a guy. Herbie was a guy. That little dog seriously needed some guy time, and I was his man.

"Let me hold him," I said.

"No," Alfreeda said and laughed. "He wants me, see?"

She made his front leg wave. "That's it, Herbie, sweetie," she said in that weird talking-to-babies voice. "Wave bye-bye. Your mommy's driving away. Look! Zoom! There she goes!"

Right away, Herbie started to cry quiet little cries. Lots of them, one right on top of the other. His stomach went in and out with every cry, like waves in a kiddie pool.

"What'd you do that for?" I demanded. "You made him watch his mom leave? You made him cry!"

"Alfie," she said in her teacher voice. "What do *you* do every time Dad leaves for Up North, huh? You won't let Mom leave the airport! Not till Dad's plane is a speck in the sky!"

That shut me up.

But Herbie kept crying. Fast little cries. Bunches of them. They sure were squeaky. Like a baby mouse that's lost in a corn maze and can't find its mommy.

Truth is, that's pretty much the way I feel whenever Dad leaves. On the first day, anyhow. But that's beside the point.

"*Shh*, Herbie Boo Boo," Alfreeda said and rocked him. "You'll be just fine. You and I, we'll have lots of fun. You'll see!"

She marched to Herbie's pen. I followed. She put Herbie on top of his little bed and covered him with the little Hound Hotel blanket. She made sure his head was on the little pillow. His nose bumped the treat, but he didn't even sniff it. He didn't even move. He just kept crying.

I couldn't stand seeing him like that, so I ran to the storeroom and found a little red ball. I ran back with it and dropped it on the floor, right in front of his bed. Herbie didn't even lift his chin. I caught the ball as it bounced and dropped it again.

Alfreeda rolled her eyes. "Stop that," she said.

"No!" I bounced the ball again. "Come on, pal. Let's play!"

Herbie stared at the teensy bone treat. I couldn't believe he wouldn't eat it.

I bounced the ball again.

Alfreeda rolled her eyes again. I wished those eyes would roll right out of her head and down a drain.

"So, Alfie," she said in her teacher voice. "What do *you* feel like doing, right after Dad leaves, huh?"

"Well, um, lie around, I guess," I said. "And sleep."

And cry sometimes, I thought.

"Exactly," she said.

She picked up Herbie. She wrapped the blanket around him. She rocked him and started to sing, "Twinkle, twinkle, little star."

Herbie kept right on crying.

"He needs to get outside," I said.

"Not yet," Alfreeda said. "He needs to feel sad first. That's right, honey. Go ahead and cry."

She rocked him and sang, "Mary had a little lamb . . ." Man, that poor dog. I was feeling sorrier for him by the second!

"Okay," I said. "I'll get him unpacked. Then we're going outside."

I grabbed the puny suitcase. It was baby blue and had little sparkly puppies all over it.

I unzipped it and pulled out a baby-blue doggie sweater. It had sparkly purple letters on the front that said, "My heart belongs to Mommy!"

Gross! I dropped it on the floor.

"Ooh, you'll look too cute in that, Herbie Boo Boo," Alfreeda cooed.

Herbie didn't answer. Not just because he's a dog and can't talk, but because he'd fallen asleep in Alfreeda's arms.

She kept rocking him. She started to sing, super quiet, "Row, row, row your boat . . ."

I unpacked the rest of Herbie's junk. I couldn't believe my eyeballs.

Ms. Frill had sent baby food for him. That's right. Like for human babies. In teensy jars . . . fruit . . . veggies.

"Whoa," I said. "That's really weird."

Alfreeda's eyebrows went up. She didn't say anything.

"Come on," I said. "Don't tell me that isn't weird."

She still didn't say anything.

Ha. Had her there.

Next, I pulled out a doggie chew toy. It was shaped like a baby bottle. I. Am. Not. Kidding.

"Weird!" I said and tossed it across the pen.

Then I pulled out something creepy.

"Ew!" I said. "What's this thing?"

Truth is, I knew what it was: a lady's nightgown!

"Disgusting!" I threw it over my shoulder and shivered.

"*Shh*," Alfreeda said. "You'll wake him up. And for your information, Ms. Frill sent that because it *smells* like her. It will make Herbie will feel more at home."

"Who cares?" I said. "A lady's nightgown is still gross!"

I dug to the bottom of the suitcase.

"What?" I said. "No more toys?"

The last thing was a picture of Ms. Frill in a fancy frame.

Alfreeda looked at it. Suddenly she put Herbie in my arms. "Hold him," she ordered. "Don't wake him up. I'll be back soon." She dashed out of the kennel room.

I stared at the furry-faced little guy in my arms. Man, he was cute.

I started to wish that I had a Yorkie. One of my own. One I could keep in my room, away from Alfreeda.

But my dad has a thing against little dogs. He likes his dogs big like wolves.

That's why Mom had started Hound Hotel. She was crazy about all sorts of dogs — big, little, and everything in between. She loved them all, and one or two family dogs would never be enough.

"Where did that silly Alfreeda go to, *hmm?*" I asked in a voice as soft as his silky hair.

I started to rock him, back and forth, like a tree branch rocks on a windy day.

I started to sing, "Down at the station, early in the morning . . ."

My voice came out wrong. Kind of like a howling beagle. Herbie woke right up. His super-cute eyes opened wide. He lifted his little head. He looked around. I could tell he didn't know where in the world he was.

Then man, he started to cry *super* loud!

CHAPTER 4
Come On, Little Dude

A minute later, Alfreeda dashed into Herbie's pen. The little guy was crying his lungs out.

"What did you *do* to him?" she demanded.

"Nothing!" I said.

She was carrying a little purple table. It came from her bedroom. Normally, she kept some of her stuffed dogs on it. She had hundreds.

She put the table in the corner and sat
Ms. Frill's picture on top of it. Then she took
Herbie from me.

"It's okay, baby," she cooed in his ear.

"He is *not* a baby," I said.

"Well, Alfie," Alfreeda said in her school
principal voice, "his mom treats him like one.
So *we* have to. Then he'll feel more at home.
Get it?"

She had a point.

"Look, Herbie!" Alfreeda pointed at Ms.
Frill's picture. "There's your mommy! Just look
at her whenever you feel sad. She's right here
with you!"

Herbie stared at the picture. He was totally
quiet.

"Told you," Alfreeda said to me. "No more crying."

Herbie kept staring at his mom. I looked at him.

Then my mouth must've fallen open because Alfreeda said, "What?"

I pointed at Herbie. "Whoa," I said. "I've *never* seen a dog do that."

My sister and I looked closer.

The little guy was crying. But I mean, for real.

I mean, he had real tears! Wet ones! The hair under his eyes was getting *wet*!

"That's it," I said. I took Herbie from Alfreeda. "Come on, little dude. We're going outside."

🐾 🐾 🐾

I figured some fresh air would do the little dude some good. And maybe a game of catch. Anything to get his mind off his mom.

That's the kind of thing my mom says to me whenever Dad leaves. And what do I usually do? Roll over in my bed and pull a pillow over my head. But that's beside the point. It was time for Herbie to get a life.

I carried him out to the play yard. That's a big fenced-in place for the dogs. It's real grassy and full of dog toys. It even has a dog slide and dog pool. Really, they're for toddlers — human ones — but only dogs go in ours.

I put Herbie on the grass and grabbed a Frisbee. I threw it. Not hard. Not far.

"Come on, Herb!" I said. "Go get it!" It should have been super easy for him to catch. But did he even try?

He didn't even sit up. He didn't even look at the Frisbee.

He stared at a rock.

"Come on, bud." I propped up his back legs.

He plopped back down. He just sat on his rear and didn't move.

"Want to go down the slide?" I asked. "I'll help you up. You'll go zooming down! It's a blast! Come on!"

He started to cry all over again!

Fast, loud cries. Like a crying machine with a power motor.

I used to cry like that when I was little. And maybe even now when I get really upset.

(Like whenever Dad would leave for Up North to study the wolves.)

Alfreeda kneeled beside us. She stared at Herbie. I stared at him, too.

Then I stared at my sister. She's never that quiet.

Right away, she started to look weird. Her eyes got all sparkly. She looked like she'd just seen a really bright light turn on, right over her head. That meant she had an idea.

I thought, *Uh-oh. Here we go again.*

CHAPTER 5
Hold Your Horseys Now, Pardner

Alfreeda didn't lose a second. She picked Herbie right up and carried him inside the kennel building. I followed.

"What are doing?" I demanded. "He was just about to fetch the Frisbee."

"Right," she said. "Like you get over it right away when Dad leaves. I always suggest fun stuff to do and you always say, 'Go away.'" She laughed.

"It's not funny," I said.

"I know it isn't," she said. "I take that laugh back. Stay with him. I'll be back soon."

She took off.

Herbie stared at his mom's picture. He just kept sobbing.

Man, this was no fun.

I stared at the dogs in the other pens. I could've been playing with a beagle. Or a bulldog.

Or a huge furry wolfhound! I looked at that big dog and started to think. *That big guy and I, we could play prehistory stuff. I could be the caveman. He could be the wooly mammoth . . . No! I can't ditch Herbie. He needs me!*

I started to pat Herbie, real gentle. He kept right on crying, like his teensy heart was cracked in half.

"*Shh*, bud," I said. "It's okay. You'll see your mom in only three days. Then you can tell her all about the blast you had here!"

Herbie stopped crying. He looked at me. He tilted his head.

It's like he was asking me, "Blast? What blast?"

I nodded and said, "You're right, pal. Let's get this party started. First, let's get rid of this junk."

Fast as a greyhound at a racetrack, I put his mom's picture into his suitcase. Then the baby food jars and the bib.

"We serve guy chow at this here country café, bud," I said in my best cowboy voice.

Then I took off his hair bow, his baby shirt, and his collar. I dropped them in the suitcase. I tossed in the sick baby-bottle chew thing,

too. I didn't touch the nightgown. *Ew.* Then I
zipped the zipper and carried the suitcase to
the storeroom. I left it there.

I went back to Herbie and said, "Cool, man.
Look, you're a normal guy dog now. See?"

I dumped the water out of his water dish.
I turned it upside down. Instant mirror. "Look,"
I said.

Herbie stared at himself. Then I couldn't
believe my eardrums.

He yipped! I'm saying, he *yipped*!

A happy-dog yip!

He put his nose right up to the shiny metal.
He pawed at the dog dish. Hard. Man, that
little guy had some guns. The dish flew across
the pen. It hit the chain-link fence then banged
on the floor. Right away, Herbie started to cry
again.

Fast as a runaway horse, I began talking in my cowboy voice again. "Whoa there, little dude. Hold your horseys now, pardner. I'll go find my little old horsey on wheels. I'll take you on a wild ride around this here ranch, okie doke? Be right back."

I dashed outside and into our garage. I dug and dug and tossed and threw. I couldn't find my little old horsey on wheels anywhere! Finally, I gave up and headed back to Herbie's pen.

I took one look around then shouted at my sister, "What did you *do* to this place?"

Alfreeda grinned at me. "Like it?" she asked. "It's Herbie's baby nursery."

All of the junk was back out of Herbie's suitcase. But that's not all. The pen was packed with stuffed dogs. She'd brought down my old blue high chair too. You know, the kind babies

sit in to eat. Herbie was sitting in
it. I stared at him.

I couldn't believe my
eyeballs. "Where
did you get that?" I
demanded.

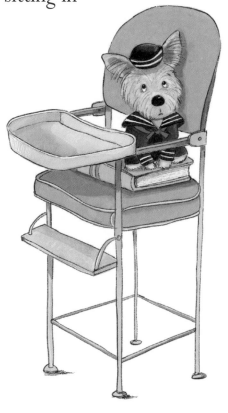

Herbie was wearing
a teensy sailor suit. It
had a matching shirt,
pants, and hat. I had
to admit that Herbie
looked super cute. But
that's beside the point.
That was *my* sailor suit!
I'd seen it in my baby
pictures!

"Come on, where'd you find it?" I
demanded.

"In the attic!" Alfreeda said and grinned

wider. "I couldn't believe it. I found all our baby stuff up there! I didn't know Mom and Dad had kept it!"

Suddenly, I'd had enough. "Hey," I said.

"What?" she said.

"Any clue how old Herbie is?" I asked.

She shook her head.

"He's six!" I shouted. "I read his information form! Six people years! How many *dog* years is that?"

"Um," she said, "let's see. Six times seven. Okay, um. Forty-two?"

Man, how could she do that math so fast?

I had no idea if forty-two was the right answer. But I acted like it was.

"That's right!" I said. "He's *not* a baby! Stop

treating him like one, or he'll hate it here! His mommy will be able to tell. She'll never bring him back!"

That shut my sister right up.

"Hold tight, Herb, old boy," I said. "Alfie will be right back to save the day."

Then I ran to the house and up to the attic.

I was going to find my horsey on wheels!

CHAPTER 6
The Alfie Male

"Man, Alfreeda made a mess up here," I said.

I was talking to my horsey on wheels. I held him in my arms.

My sister had dumped out tons of boxes, and stuff covered the attic floor.

"Mom's going to make her clean this up," I said. "I guess Alfreeda won't care anyway. She does everything super fast. I hate that!"

Horsey didn't say anything. Take it from me.

Friendship with a stuffed toy only goes so far. I kicked stuff out of the way, trying to get back to the door.

Suddenly I spied something. Two things, I mean. Two teensy baby T-shirts. One pink, one blue.

The pink one said, "ALFREEDA FEMALE."

The blue one said, "ALFIE MALE."

"Was I really that little once?" I asked Horsey. "Man, I must've been cute in that tiny shirt."

I read the words out loud, "Alfie Male."

Suddenly it hit me. Something I'd never thought about before.

ALFIE MALE. Get it? As in, "Alpha Male."

ALFREEDA FEMALE. Get it? Yeah! "Alpha Female."

Trust my parents to do something that weird.

See, every wolf pack in the world has them. A boy leader and a girl leader. "Alpha" means "first" or "top." As in, "top dog."

The Alpha Male and Alpha Female are the biggest, smartest, bravest, strongest wolves in their pack. And yeah, the fastest. They take care of their whole pack.

"Know what, Horsey?" I said. "I think my parents wanted my sister and me to be born leaders. Both of us. Not just the one born five minutes before me."

I gave Horsey a good pet up and down his nose.

"Buck up, old boy," I said in my cowboy voice. "It's time to show a little dude a wild good time on this here ranch. Giddyup!"

I grabbed my old baby cowboy hat off the floor. Then I dashed to the kennels, as fast as a wild pony, bolting over the plains.

CHAPTER 7

Ride 'Em, Little Cowdog!

Two minutes later, Alfreeda took one look at Horsey and rolled her eyes.

"No way," she said. "Herbie's *not* going for a horseback ride. He'll fall right off that thing!"

She had a point.

She also had the one of the world's fastest brains.

She snapped her fingers. "I'll make a saddle!" she said.

In about four minutes flat, she had a cardboard saddle all rigged up. It was tied up nice and tight with lots of tape.

She patted the finished saddle. "Ride 'em, Little Cowdog!" she said in her cowgirl voice.

Then I couldn't believe my eyeballs. Herbie jumped right onto the saddle!

"Yee-haw!" I said. "Giddyup!" And Herbie started to ride horseback from room to room. I pushed. Alfreeda galloped along on her hands and knees, right beside us.

And get this: The cool little cowdog didn't just sit on that saddle. He stood on his back legs and put his front paws on top of Horsey's head!

"Now you can see the whole ranch, little dude," I said, panting as I pushed. "Get out there and check your cows. Make sure no wolves got 'em in the night. Giddyup!"

We galloped right past Mom. She was talking to some guests in the office. We galloped through all the rooms again. Herbie barked and barked. Like the happiest cowdog in the whole Wild West!

"If only your mommy could see you now!" Alfreeda cried.

We galloped through the office again, down the hallway, and right past Mom.

Mom was leading a little Maltese named Muffin toward her pen. Muffin had stayed with us before.

"Hi, Muffin!" I called as I galloped by.

"Welcome back, Muffin!" Alfreeda said, galloping fast.

Suddenly, Herbie leaped off the saddle.

"Whoa, Horsey!" I cried. "We've lost our rider!"

Alfreeda and I stopped. We looked back. There stood Herbie, nose to nose with Muffin. Old Herb was wagging his tail like crazy.

CHAPTER 8
Baby-Blue-Sky Day

Five minutes later, Horsey sat in a corner of the storeroom. Alfreeda and I were out in the play yard. So were the two new little best buds.

They kept rolling around and running in circles. And chasing each other's tails. And jumping on top of each other. Herbie kept yipping that happy-dog yip.

I sighed. Then I tried again to throw the ball. "Come on, Herb, old boy," I called. "Catch it! Bring it to me!"

It was like he'd forgotten I was even alive. I sure hoped my dad wouldn't forget about me, being away for a whole month and all.

I went over to the big old maple tree. Alfreeda was lying under it in the shade. I sat beside her.

"This is so boring," she said. "If only we had another horse Muffin could ride."

"Yeah." A fly landed on my nose. I blew it away. A cow mooed somewhere.

"I guess Herbie really likes playing with another small dog," I said.

Alfreeda sat up fast. "What's the matter with him?" she demanded. "Aren't we good enough?"

"We're kids, not dogs," I said.

"Sometimes I forget that," she said.

Suddenly I snapped my fingers. "Hey!" I said.

"Maybe that's what Herbie saw in the mirror! I mean, the bottom of his water dish! He thought he saw another little dog to play with!"

Alfreeda wrinkled up her face. "What are you talking about?" she said. "You're weird, Alfie Wolfe."

"You're weirder, Alfreeda Wolfe," I said.

That same stupid fly landed on my nose again. I swatted it away. A chicken clucked somewhere.

I started to think. *I guess that's what I need the most too when Dad is gone. A friend to play with.*

Too bad there weren't any friends around our place. All of mine lived in town.

"It's hot," Alfreeda said.

"We could fill up the dog pool," I said. "My old baby boat is in the attic."

"We could turn the boat into a pirate ship," she said.

"How about we dress Herbie up like a pirate?" I asked. "He'd fit right in that little boat."

"We could dress Muffin up too," she said. "Like a girl pirate. We could use our old baby bathtub for a pirate ship. Both dogs would fit in that."

"Cool," I said.

Alfreeda jumped up.

"Watch them," she said in her top-dog voice. "Fill the pool. I'll go get the pirate gear."

"Aye, matey," I said in my pirate voice. It was growly and tough and from the gut.

"Hey, grab my pirate costume, too," I said. "I'll be Captain Hook."

"No!" she said. "I want to!" My sister and I both dressed up like Captain Hook one Halloween.

Right then, something really weird happened. I couldn't believe my eyeballs.

Nice and slow, Alfreeda shrugged. Then I couldn't believe my eardrums. "Okay," she said. "You can be Captain."

I jumped up and got busy filling the little kiddie pool. Herbie and Muffin ran right over to me. I held the hose high, letting them drink from the stream.

Suddenly it felt like a sunshiny, baby-blue-sky day. I let out a happy howl, like a wolf calling to the sunshine-yellow moon.

"Know what, Herb and Muff?" I said. "I sure hope my dad's having as much fun Up North! Hop in, little guys. The water's fine!"

Is a Yorkshire Terrier the Dog for You?

Hi! It's me, Alfreeda!

I bet you want your own teeny, tiny, super-cute Yorkie now too, right? Of course you do! But actually, Yorkies make good pets for only some families. So before you dash off to buy or adopt one, here are some important facts you should know:

Yorkies are toy-size dogs and have teeny bones, ones that break easily**.** Tripping over a Yorkie, or sitting on him by accident, can spell B-I-G trouble for such a little dog. If you have young kids in your family, get a bigger dog that can handle lots of wild kid action.

Yorkies can be hard to housebreak. (That means getting them to go to the bathroom outside.) Yorkies HATE cold or rainy days. If you live where it's really cold or rainy a lot, your Yorkie might not go outside to do her business. (Some families use an indoor litter box or a small doggy door leading to a covered potty yard.)

Yorkies HAVE to be brushed or combed every day, and their hair needs cutting often, too. Their hair is fine and straight, so it gets messy fast. If you can't promise to brush your dog every day, don't get a Yorkie. Get a hamster.

Okay, signing off for now . . . until the next adventure at Hound Hotel!

Yours very factually,

Alfreeda Wolfe

Glossary

annoying (uh-NOI-ing)—making someone lose patience or feel angry

canyon (KAN-yuhn)—a deep, narrow river valley with steep sides

creatures (KREE-churs)—living beings, human or animal

crooked (KRUK-id)—not straight

demanded (di-MAN-ded)—asked or called for with authority

disgusting (diss-GUHSS-ting)—very unpleasant and offensive to others

fetched (FECHED)—went after and brought back something or somebody

galloped (GAL-uhpd)—ran fast

howling (HOU-ling)—making a loud, sad noise

overflowing (OH-vur-floh-ing)—flowing over the edges of something

puny (PYOO-nee)—small and weak, or unimportant

shoved (SHUHVD)—pushed hard or roughly

sparkly (SPAR-klee)—shiny or glittery

Talk About It

1. Which character do you think you are most like and why?

2. What would be the pros and cons of living next to a dog-boarding kennel?

3. On page 68, Alfreeda has shared some facts (and opinions) about Yorkshire terriers. Do you think a Yorkshire terrier would be a good dog for your family? Why or why not?

Write About It

1. Think about a time you felt homesick. Write a paragraph or two comparing how you felt to the way Herbie seems to feel in the story.

2. Write a letter to the twins' dad about Herbie. Use either Alfie's or Alfreeda's point of view.

3. Write a research paper on Yorkshire terriers. Use three or more sources.

About the Author

Shelley Swanson Sateren grew up with five pet dogs — a beagle, a terrier mix, a terrier-poodle mix, a Weimaraner, and a German shorthaired pointer. As an adult, she adopted a lively West Highland white terrier named Max. Besides having written many children's books, Shelley has worked as a children's book editor and in a children's bookstore. She lives in Saint Paul, Minnesota, with her husband, and has two grown sons.

About the Illustrator

Deborah Melmon has worked as an illustrator for over 25 years. After graduating from Academy of Art University in San Francisco, she started her career illustrating covers for the *Palo Alto Weekly* newspaper. Since then, she has produced artwork for over twenty children's books. Her artwork can also be found on giftwrap, greeting cards, and fabric. Deborah lives in Menlo Park, California, and shares her studio with an energetic Airedale Terrier named Mack.

THE FUN DOESN'T STOP HERE!

Discover more at
www.capstonekids.com

VIDEOS & CONTESTS
GAMES & PUZZLES
FRIENDS & FAVORITES
AUTHORS & ILLUSTRATORS

Find cool websites and more books like this one at **www.facthound.com**

Just type in the Book ID: 9781479558971 and you're ready to go!